Hello, Family Members,

Learning to read is one of the most important accomplishments of early childhood. **Hello Reader!** books are designed to help children become skilled readers who like to read. Beginning readers learn to read by remembering frequently used words like "the," "is," and "and"; by using phonics skills to decode new words; and by interpreting picture and text clues. These books provide both the stories children enjoy and the structure they need to read fluently and independently. Here are suggestions for helping your child *before*, *during*, and *after* reading:

Before

- Look at the cover and pictures and have your child predict what the story is about.
- Read the story to your child.
- Encourage your child to chime in with familiar words and phrases.
- Echo read with your child by reading a line first and having your child read it after you do.

During

- Have your child think about a word he or she does not recognize right away. Provide hints such as "Let's see if we know the sounds" and "Have we read other words like this one?"
- Encourage your child to use phonics skills to sound out new words.
- Provide the word for your child when more assistance is needed so that he or she does not struggle and the experience of reading with you is a positive one.
- Encourage your child to have fun by reading with a lot of expression . . . like an actor!

After

- Have your child keep lists of interesting and favorite words.
- Encourage your child to read the books over and over again. Have him or her read to brothers, sisters, grandparents, and even teddy bears. Repeated readings develop confidence in young readers.
- Talk about the stories. Ask and answer questions. Share ideas about the funniest and most interesting characters and events in the stories.

I do hope that you and your child enjoy this book.

—Francie Alexander
  Reading Specialist,
  Scholastic's Instructional Publishing Group

To Sarah
— H.W.

Go to www.scholastic.com for Web site information on
Scholastic authors and illustrators.

Copyright © 1999 by Hans Wilhelm, Inc.
All rights reserved. Published by Scholastic Inc.
SCHOLASTIC, HELLO READER! and CARTWHEEL BOOKS and associated logos
are trademarks and/or registered trademarks of Scholastic Inc.

Library of Congress Cataloging-in-Publication Data
Wilhelm, Hans, 1945-
    I lost my tooth! / by Hans Wilhelm.
        p.   cm. — (Hello reader! Level 1)
    "Cartwheel books."
    Summary: When Puppy's tooth comes out and he loses it, he figures out a
way to get treats from the Tooth Fairy anyway.
    ISBN 0-590-64230-8
    [1. Dogs—Fiction. 2. Tooth Fairy—Fiction. 3. Teeth—Fiction]
    I. Title. II. Series.
PZ7.W64816Iag   1999
[E]—dc21   98-3668
                                                                        CIP
                                                                         AC
12 11 10 9 8 7 6 5 4 3 2 1   9/9 0/0 01 02 03 04
                        Printed in the U.S.A.   24
                        First printing, February 1999

I LOST MY TOOTH!

by Hans Wilhelm

Hello Reader! — Level 1

SCHOLASTIC INC.
Cartwheel BOOKS®

New York   Toronto   London   Auckland   Sydney

Look, everyone! Look what I have!

I have a loose tooth.

When it falls out, I will put it under my pillow. The Tooth Fairy will give me a treat.

Now I am hungry.

That tastes yummy.

Oh, no!

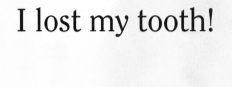

I lost my tooth!

What will I do?

I have an idea!

There is the camera!

I will take a picture.

Here it comes.

It looks great!

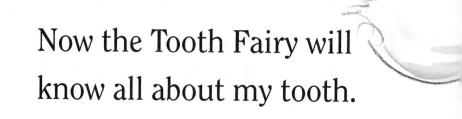

Now the Tooth Fairy will
know all about my tooth.

I hope she comes tonight.

Yes, she was here!
I got my treats!

I wonder which tooth
will be next.